Written by

Fiona Miller

PETE

For my funny, happy children, Seth and Sinead, who have
had to wear glasses since a very young age!

This is Pete. Say 'Hi PETE!'

Pete has a little problem. He BUMPS into a lot of things.

Sometimes Pete FALLS in things too.

He often finds himself swimming
into the wrong things.

And he is always ruining things
while children are playing.

But Pete's **BiGGEST** problem is that he steps in disgusting things.

What should Pete do?

Well, first things first, Pete is going for an EYE TEST.

Guess what? Pete needs glasses!
What do YOU think?

Pete is very happy with
his new glasses.

He is so happy, he is
DANCiNG around.

He should watch out though, as he is
very close to the edge of a CLIFF...

Well, that is the end of Pete!

Only kidding, he is just below the water

SWiMMiNG happily with

the beautiful fish.

Say 'Hi FiSH!'

He is enjoying playing with his
friends too.

And he never steps in
anything BAD...

Or **ALMOST** never!

Printed in Great Britain
by Amazon